Hartland Public Library

Hartland, WI 53029

THE SECRET KNOCK CLUB #4

THE GREAT SLEEP-UNDER

By Louise Bonnett-Rampersaud
Pictures by Adam McCauley

two lions

two lions

Text copyright © 2016 Louise Bonnett-Rampersaud
Illustrations copyright © 2016 by Adam McHeffey
All rights reserved.

Published by Two Lions, New York

www.apub.com

Amazon, the Amazon logo, and Two Lions are trademarks of Amazon.com, Inc., or its affiliates.

ISBN-13: 9781503950634
ISBN-10: 1503950638

Book design by Lindsey Andrews

Printed in the United States of America

To Richard, 1965–2014. Love, forever.

Contents

CHAPTER 1

"WHAT KIND DO YOU WANT?"

"What kind of *what?*" Heather Kellogg asked.

We were in the cubby area, hanging up our stuff before class started.

"Nickname," I said. I stared into her eyeballs. "Just because our school lost the spelling bee last week doesn't mean we're not going to win *something* soon. I can feel it! And when we win, we'll become famous, and when you're famous, it's good to have a nickname. Something catchy that people will remember you by."

I looked into her Kellogg eyeballs again, thinking. "That's it! You have a cereal name, so you should have a cereal nickname. You know, *Kellogg.*" I opened my backpack and pulled out some paper. "I can't believe we never thought of this before!"

I eyed her up and down. "How about Froot Loop?" I wrote it down.

Her cereal mouth did not answer.

"Okay, you could be one of the Flakes, then. Corn *or* Frosted. Your choice." I smiled.

But just then Mrs. Duncan started calling us over to our desks. To start the important part of the day.

Only here's the thing.

Cereal nicknames for when you become famous *are* important!

"Quick," I shouted. I started talking faster. "Corn Pop? Apple Jack? Rice Krispy?"

Fudgy walked by. "No thanks," he said, rubbing his stomach. "I already had breakfast." He laughed and high-fived The Cape.

They walked to their seats.

Heather followed them, ignoring me.

With her real-alive, unfamous name!

What I learned today:

Trying to help a friend become ready for fame is very hard!

"Class," Mrs. Duncan said, "we have a

lot of things to cover today, so let's put our thinking caps on so we can get started and learn, learn, learn!"

Only here's the problem.

I don't have a thinking *cap*.

I have a thinking *cat*: Rat-A-Tat, who is *not* . . . I repeat . . . *not* allowed in school.

That one time Rat-A-Tat DID come to school!

I looked up at the board.

Today was a science day.

In third grade you don't do science every day. Just reading and math.

Too much science must not be good for you!

Mrs. Duncan clapped her hands together. "For Mrs. Elliott's science class today, you'll be going down to the all-purpose room to see the finalists for the science fair! We've kept it all a surprise until now. The winner from our school will be announced tomorrow night at the Science Stars event, but you'll be able to get a sneak peek at the finalists today."

She looked around the classroom.

"One lucky student will move on and represent Lakeview Elementary at the regional competition next week."

I realized two things when she said that news:

Mrs. Duncan has a doughnut-sounding name!

And we were having a walk-around learning day. My favorite kind!

Walk-around learning is when you walk around and touch things and move things and smell things, and all the learning stuff gets into your brain after visiting the rest of your body.

It's better than sit-down learning, where the learning stuff has to go straight to your brain. (And it doesn't always stay there!)

"But first," Mrs. Duncan continued, "let's figure out who's here today and who's not."

She pulled out her class list.

"Agnes is here," she said, without even having to look up.

4

Mrs. Duncan has magical powers.

She went over the rest of the list. "It looks like the only one absent is . . ." She looked at the list again and then stopped. "Oh, no, that's right," she said under her breath. "He's already down at the . . ."

I looked around the room.

Fudgy was here.

The Cape was here.

Skipper was here.

Who isn't here?

And where is he?

Already down at the . . . ?

I bonked my head!

Was somebody from our class a science fair finalist?

And then I realized something.

This was it!

This was our chance to be famous!

And not just our whole school. But our *class*.

Which was even better.

We could be Mrs. Duncan's Famous Room Five Science Stars!

I continued scanning.

And found the empty desk.
Where Sam Nash sits.
Sam Nash who suddenly had a new name.

I wrote it down in my notebook.

Super Sam the Science Star.

I smiled a happy Agnes smile at Sam's desk.

'Cause Sam was our ticket to fame, that's why!

CHAPTER 2

"ONE, TWO, THREE, EYES ON ME," MRS. DUNCAN said.

"One, two, eyes on you," we answered back.

We looked at Mrs. Duncan's important-announcement eyes.

And then her important-announcement mouth said, "I know you're all excited about the science fair, but first we have to get through some math, so let's try to stay focused."

And I did stay focused.

On my fortune-teller, that is.

"Pick a number," I whispered to Emma.

"Maybe I should have made myself a little clearer," Mrs. Duncan said, staring at the paper in my hands. "Let's try to stay focused on *math*."

I got embarrassed hands.

And put my fortune-teller in my desk.

Even though Emma was about to marry a prince and have seven children!

Her life was ruined!

Mrs. Duncan tapped the clipboard in her hand.

"Now then," she said, pointing to the back of the room. "We have some new math centers, so I want to take a minute to explain them. Station one is Fraction Action, where you will multiply and divide fractions. Station two is for practicing your multiplication tables . . ."

And here's some advice about those words.

Do not write multiplication problems on real-alive tables and say "Ta-da! A multiplication table!" when you're done. You will be sent to the principal's office and have to clean the table with soap and water and possibly spill water all over your brand-new jeans. The ones with the glittery stuff on the pockets.

Or at least I've *heard* that's what could happen.

Mrs. Duncan called our groups. Heather, Fudgy, and I were in the Fraction Action center.

The good thing about going to centers is you don't have to do a lot of work because your teacher's eyeballs are busy with another group!

I grabbed a piece of paper and wrote down:

10 THINGS TO DO WHEN YOU'RE FAMOUS

1. Call the local newspaper person.

2. Set up an interview.

3. Buy new pen for signing autographs.

I was about to write down number 4 when Mrs. Duncan's eyeballs looked up. "I think I see a lot of action over there, but I'm not sure it's *fraction* action," she said.

We were the "over there" part.

I grabbed the Fraction Action paper. And multiplied numerators. And denominators. And simplified my answers.

And let me tell you something!

There is a *lot* of action going on with fractions. They are exhausting!

There was also a lot of action going on in my head.

I had Super Sam the Science Star lighting up my brain.

"Have you heard of Bill Nye the Science Guy?" I whispered to Fudgy and Heather.

"Of course," Heather said.

"Duh," Fudgy said. "Who hasn't? 'Bill! Bill! Bill! Bill! Science rules!'" He looked at me. "That's the theme song!"

"Well, guess what? We have our own real-alive science star right here in this class! Our own Room Five Lakeview Elementary guy."

They looked around to spot the Lakeview Elementary guy.

"Well, not right *now*," I said. "He's busy being sciencey down the hall in the all-purpose room. And he's going to make us famous!"

"Who?" Fudgy asked. "*Who* is?" He got a flustered Fudgy face. "Famous? *What* are you talking about, Agnes?"

"Super Sam," I said, pointing to his desk.

"*Super* Sam?" Fudgy said, laughing. "Who's *Super* Sam?" He looked over at the desk. "You mean Sam *Nash*? He blows his nose to the tune of the national anthem, Agnes. The last time I checked that doesn't exactly make you famous. I mean *I* think it's pretty cool, but—"

11

"That's the one!" I said.

"Well, how's he *super*, then?" Heather asked.

"Wait," Skipper said. "The Sam you haven't talked to because he didn't invite you to his birthday party last month, even though he only invited boys . . ."

"Yeah, but he was making that cool slime . . ." I stopped myself. "Anyway that was so last month of me. It's not important anymore, because that was before . . ."

"Before what?"

I looked at the clock.

We had five minutes left until we switched for science.

"Just wait," I said. "You'll see." I smiled and grabbed my science notebook. "Trust me. Things are about to change."

And then I possibly imagined that the hallways of the school were lined in red carpet.

CHAPTER 3

"Sam! Sam! Sam!" I waved my hands at him and ran over to his display when we got to the all-purpose room.

Sam looked up and saw me coming.

He had a tri-fold display on his table.

He looked like he was trying to hide be-hind it.

I waved at everyone

else. "Guys. Come here!" I shouted. "Come and see Super Sam's stuff."

We all stood around and stared.

Super Sam looked super scared.

Just then Mrs. Elliott, our science teacher, stood up on the stage. She tapped the microphone. "If I could have your attention for a moment before you explore the finalists' projects. This is a very exciting time for us all at Lakeview Elementary. First, I want to congratulate all the finalists for their hard work and dedication."

I winked at Sam when she said those words.

She continued. "As you know, we will be hosting the Science Stars event tomorrow night, right here in this very room. Finalists from grades three through five will be displaying their projects, and only one lucky winner from our school will go on to regionals next week. But for now, please take the time to view our school's contributions and enjoy yourselves."

"Cool!" Fudgy said, reaching for one of the bowls on Sam's table. "Food!"

I looked closer at the display.

And saw the words *How Much Iron Does Your Breakfast Cereal Really Have? Ironing Out the Facts.*

"No!" I said, pulling Fudgy's hand away. "I think that's part of the experiment."

"Eating cereal is science?" Fudgy said, laughing. "Then cool. I must be a super scientist, too." He put his hand out for me to shake it. "Nice to meet you," he joked. "Super scientist at your service."

I apologized to Sam for Fudgy's behavior. "He doesn't know how to be a true fan of your work," I said, blushing. "This looks amazing to me!" I added. "I think you're definitely going to win and be famous!" I stepped back to get a better look. "What exactly is it?"

There were four bowls on Sam's table. Each one had a different type of cereal in it. There were also a blender and funnels made from plastic bottles with magnets duct-taped to the outside.

It looked like a crime scene!

Heather picked up one of the bottles. "What's the magnet for?" she asked, poking the bottom of the bottle.

"The bottle is magnetized to catch the iron . . ."

"Magnet eyes?" I said. "Cool." I nodded to everyone standing around me to make Sam even more famous. "This *is* an awesome experiment."

Sam shook his head.

And his hands.

"No, I said it was magne*tized* . . ."

But it was too late!

Skipper and The Cape pushed their way forward. "What? Magnet eyes? Let *us* see." They made an announcement to the all-purpose room. "Everyone. Over here. He's got magnet eyes. You've *got* to see."

Pretty soon everyone was standing around Sam's table looking for the magnet eyes.

Super Sam looked super red!

"What's *that*?" a fourth grader said, pointing to his tri-fold. "What's that stuff hanging in plastic wrap?"

Sam turned to look. "Oh, that?" he said, getting a little less red. "Those are iron pellets collected from the cereal."

The fourth grader spoke up. "Wait. I couldn't hear him," she said. "Did he say pellets? As in *rabbit* pellets? That's disgusting! That's poop!" She ran away from the table, screaming. "Yuck!!!! Rabbit poop! Run!"

Suddenly there was rabbit-pellet panic.

Plus also, there was Principal Not-Such-A-Joy standing at the door.

"Come back, everybody!" I yelled. "He didn't say *rabbit* pellets. He said *iron* pellets. There's no poop!"

Nobody came back.

"What's going on in here?" Principal Not-Such-A-Joy said, dodging the fleeing rabbit-pellet people.

I put my hands over my eyes and shook my head. "I'm sorry, Sam!" I said.

Fudgy whispered in my ear. "At least there's one good thing," he said, laughing. "You're talking to Sam again!"

I did *not* laugh back.

CHAPTER 4

HERE IS SOME NEWS ABOUT RABBIT-PELLET panic.

It is hard to calm down.

Even for people with the title of principal.

Principal Not-Such-A-Joy told everyone to quiet down immediately.

Everyone told her there were rabbits on the loose!

And they started making rabbit ears behind each other's heads.

And possibly also behind *her* head.

Principal Not-Such-A-Joy hopped—I mean *walked*!—over to the stage. She

used her microphone voice to tell all the pellet people to quiet down again.

Then she looked over at me.

Her face said *Agnes, do you know anything about all this poop-and-pellet business?* without even talking!

Then she walked back over to Sam's table.

"I think it might be all my fault," I blurted out, before she could say anything. "I thought Sam said his experiment was magnet *eyes* . . . and before you know it . . ." I stopped and turned to Sam. "By the way, have you met Sam? How rude of me!" I reached out to give him a hug. "Sam's the best! He's basically famous."

Sam backed up.

Science people must not be the hugging kind.

Principal Not-Such-A-Joy nodded. And chuckled. "I *am* the principal of this place, Agnes. I make it a point to know all my students." She smiled at Sam and then looked down at me and winked. "But some students I get to spend a little more time with . . ." she continued. "Speaking of that, it looks like everything is under control here now, so why don't you come out in the hall with me so we can have a little chat about what just happened? I'll let Mrs. Duncan know you'll be with me for a minute."

"Wait," I said. My eyeballs lit up. "Can we go to your office instead?"

'Cause just then I had an idea that was the really great kind. I wanted to call the local newspaper reporter person who handles famous elementary classes. I mean . . . famous elementary science stars! He or she needed to come out and cover the Science Stars event tomorrow tonight!

It would be perfect for Sam's fame!

Plus also, maybe it would say "Sorry for all this rabbit-pellet mess."

Principal Not-Such-A-Joy held up her finger.

It was like a remote putting my mouth on pause.

She turned to Sam.

He was trying to tape the magnet back on to the bottle.

And put the bowls back in the right places.

"Before Agnes and I go, are you okay here?" She looked down at his table. "Your experiment is still in one piece, right?"

Sam nodded.

"Now then," she said, turning to me. "What is this about going *to* my office? Usually kids are trying to get *out* of there . . ."

"I need to use your phone," I said, jumping up and down.

"My *phone?*" She looked surprised. "Do you think you're in that much trouble?"

"Oh, no!" I said, laughing. "I need to call the newspaper." I looked up at the clock. "I just hope it's not too late."

"The newspaper?" I heard Principal Not-

Such-A-Joy say to herself. *"What on earth?"*

But it was too late to explain. The event was tomorrow! I ran down the hall ahead of her and waited outside her office.

And let me tell you something.

It is hard to be patient when you're ready to famous up a place!

CHAPTER 5

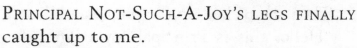

PRINCIPAL NOT-SUCH-A-JOY'S LEGS FINALLY caught up to me.

"What's the rush, Agnes?" she said, possibly a little out of breath. She was sort of bent over.

Mrs. Palmer, the secretary, handed her a note. She took it and walked into her office. "Follow me," she said, not looking up from her note.

I walked behind her.

Like a little Agnes duckling.

Principal Not-Such-A-Joy put the note down on her desk. "Now then," she said, looking over her glasses. "What's this about the newspaper?"

"I want to call it," I said. "I want to invite them to the Science Stars event. And we're running out of time!"

Principal Not-Such-A-Joy agreed. "You know what? These kids do deserve some community recognition. I think it's a great idea." She looked on her computer and found the phone number.

Then she picked up the phone and dialed.

"Hello, this is Principal Joy from Lakeview Elementary School," she began. "I have a student here who is interested in talking to the reporter who covers local elementary schools and events, please."

She nodded and gave me the thumbs-up sign. Then she put her hand over the part of the phone where the words come out.

"Go ahead and do your thing," she said, handing me the phone.

"Would you like to be a star?" I asked newspaper reporter person Ms. Ellen Marker when she got on the phone.

There is a voice you use when you talk to important newspaper people.

It is called an English accent.

It is also the voice for official Secret Knock Club business.

Only this wasn't official business.

Well, at least it wasn't *yet*!

Principal Not-Such-A-Joy had heard my accent before.

Ms. Ellen Marker hadn't. "I'm sorry," she said. "I'm not sure I'm understanding you correctly."

"Would you like to be a star?" I asked again.

"A star?"

"Yes, tomorrow tonight at Lakeview Elementary. You can be a star among stars. Science stars, that is! Seven o'clock on the dot. It's to choose the science fair winner who will go on to the regional competition next week."

She paused a moment, probably to check her calendar.

"I'm afraid I can't be a star tomorrow night, honey," she said. "That's a little too short notice for me. I'm already booked."

My famous plans were squashed like a bug!

I thought fast.

"Well, how long do you need for long notice?" I asked. "'Cause I'm sure Sam is going to make it to regionals next week, and maybe you can make us stars—I mean make *him* a famous star—then."

"That sounds wonderful," she said. "I would love to make him a famous star. When is it exactly next week so I can put it on my calendar?"

I looked at Principal Not-Such-A-Joy when she said those words and mouthed, "When?"

She pointed to the calendar.

"April seventh," I told Ms. Marker.

"April seventh it is!" she said. "Looking forward to it."

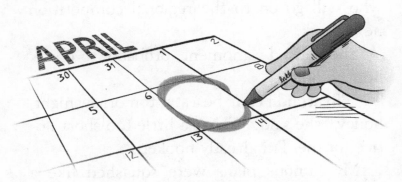

And I smiled an "Agnes-is-looking-forward-to-it-too" smile.

CHAPTER 6

"LET'S GET THIS SHOW ON THE ROAD," I SAID to Mr. Tim, our bus driver, later on that day. "Got lots to do today!"

Mr. Tim nodded his bus driver head. "Yes, ma'am," he said, laughing. "That's my Agnes. Always has something brewing."

He winked as I walked to my seat.

And it was true.

I did have a lot to do. I was going to call an emergency meeting of the SKC.

A Super Sam Special Session!

The Secret Knock Club is what we call our club for long.

SKC is what we call it for short.

But first, Kindergarten Heather was calling. "Wagnes!" she shouted. "Sit here!"

I pulled out my bus-seat towel and sat down next to her.

"Wagnes!!!" she said, grabbing my arm. She clung to it like a koala bear. Her little kindergarten body was all bouncy and jumpy, like it was popping popcorn on the inside. And her cheeks were pink and puffy. "We had cupcakes for birthday club!" she said, smiling. "I had two! With pimples on top."

I wiped her face a little. "I can tell!" I said. "But I think you mean *sprinkles*, Heather. *Sprinkles*, not pimples!"

"Yep! Pimples," she said again. "They're the best!"

Kindergartners!

Fudgy leaned across the aisle.

"At least she only has pimples," he said, laughing. "And not magnet eyes!" He and Skipper made their eyes all big and round. And pretended to look like zombies.

I pretended to look away.

"What did the principal say anyway?" Fudgy asked.

I didn't answer.

"No really, Agnes. What did she say?" Fudgy leaned across and tapped my shoulder. "When she took you to her office. Were you in *trouble*, Agnes?"

Skipper and The Cape made "ooohhh" sounds when Fudgy said those words.

I turned around. "Trouble?" I said. "No way! She let me use her phone to call the newspaper. To make Sam famous."

"*Sam? Famous?*" Fudgy rolled his zombie-magnet eyes. "What are you up to *now*, Agnes?" He looked at Skipper. And across at The Cape. "All I can say is, whatever it is, it better not include us." He nodded his head at them. "Right, guys?"

"Right," they all said.

"Well, too late," I said. "We're having an emergency meeting right after school, and Sam's going to be invited!"

They shook their SKC heads.

Then suddenly Fudgy got okay with that news. "Hey, you know what? Maybe it's not so bad, guys. Think about it. For once we'll have more boys than girls!"

Skipper nodded. "Oh yeah. Cool."

"True," The Cape said.

"And maybe he can teach us how to blow

our noses like he does!" Skipper said. "I'm sure he knows a couple more songs."

"And the cool slime," The Cape said. "We've got to make sure he brings *that*."

I shook my head.

"No!" my voice shouted. "You're missing the point . . ." Although the slime part did sound good . . .

But he was taking over my idea!

"I don't think so," Fudgy said, grabbing his backpack to get off the bus. "The point is that for once I think I agree with you, Agnes. Inviting Sam to our meeting *is* going to be great." He walked to the front of the bus. "In fact, *I'll* even call him and invite him. See you all later!"

He pretended to blow his nose as he got off the bus.

I looked out the window.

And made a mad Agnes face at him.

Only guess what?

I wasn't pretending.

CHAPTER 7

GRANDMA BLING STOOD UP FROM HER yogurt pose when I walked in the front door. "I think they should call this one downward puppy in my case," she

said, laughing. "Not downward dog. I can't get all the way down."

My sort-of-in-a-bad-mood mouth laughed.

Grandma Bling noticed and walked over to the refrigerator door. "Now let's see what will get that mouth all the way back to happy . . ."

Grandma Bling has a rule.

She says if you've got a 'tude sometimes you can fix it with food.

And it works. Especially when the food is the brownie kind!

But sometimes your 'tude comes right back when Fudgy calls to tell you he invited Sam. And Sam said yes because he thinks he's just coming to hang out. And *not* try to become a Science Star or anything.

"It's the boys," I said, putting the phone down. "They're going to ruin everything. Sam from our class is coming to our Secret Knock Club meeting today, which was great at first, but then the boys got all excited about it, too, and . . ."

"Sam?" Grandma Bling asked. "You mean the boy you've been mad at because he didn't invite you to his party or something?"

I nodded. "Yeah, but we're cool now. I mean now that he's Super Science Sam."

"Science?" Grandma Bling asked. "The class you call *sigh*-ence because you think it's so boring? *That* science?"

"Yep. That's the one." My mad face got in a better mood. "But that was this morning.

I love it now." I looked up at her Grandma Bling eyeballs. "Did you know you can get famous from science?"

She laughed. "Why, yes, I did. Let's see . . . there's Albert Einstein, Thomas Edison, Isaac Newton, Marie Curie—"

"No," I said, possibly interrupting her. "I mean like *newspaper* famous!" I grabbed my backpack and headed for the stairs. "I'll have to tell you all about it later! Right now I have a meeting to get ready for. But wait!" I said, running to get my yearbook from the living room. I turned to the page with Mrs. Simpson's class from last year and circled a picture.

"This is Sam," I said, showing Grandma Bling. I looked closer. "Actually, this is just his head. He has other parts, too, but if you see this head at the front door, please let me know!" I ran up the stairs and called out from the top, "I want to be the first person to welcome him."

"I'll be on the lookout!" she said.

"Oh, and another thing," I shouted down the stairs. "I almost forgot. Are you free tomorrow night?" I stuck my head out over the balcony and smiled an "Agnes-really-wants-to-go-to-the-Science-Stars-night-and-for-her-parents-to-have-a-date-night" smile.

"Why? What do you have up your sleeve, Agnes?"

"Nothing! See, I'm wearing a tank top." I laughed. "Can't have *anything* up my sleeve!"

And it worked!

Grandma Bling was in!

Five minutes later, I heard Grandma Bling's voice. "Ginger hair . . . freckles . . . bright, shiny eyes . . ." She was looking down at the yearbook and walking to the front door. "I think I've spotted him, Agnes. It might be time to come downstairs."

"Coming!" I ran down the stairs on excited legs. "Excuse me, excuse me. Science Sam Welcome Committee coming through," I said, opening the door.

"Sam!" I yelled, yanking him inside. "Quick!" I looked down the driveway. "Before the others get here."

Sam seemed surprised at my hello.

And possibly shaken.

Grandma Bling stepped in to help.

"*You* must be Sam," she said, reaching out to shake his hand. "I've heard so much about you!"

"Really?" Sam said. "Are you kidding?"

"Oh, don't be silly, Sam," I said. "We go *way* back." I grabbed his arm. "Such a sense of humor!" I said. "That's what I've always liked about you, Sam." I did a quick Agnes smile. "That and your Science Star talent, of course. Speaking of which . . ."

And I led him out the back door to the clubhouse.

CHAPTER 8

"Aren't you going to blindfold him?" Heather shouted from the other side of the yard. "You always used to do that to me!" She turned to close the gate behind her.

I pretended not to hear that Heather voice. It was my only chance!

"Quick!" I said to Sam. "Up the ladder!"

But Heather kept shouting.

So we kept climbing.

Then Heather started running.

So we kept climbing even more.

"Agnes," she said, "wait up! I know you can hear me."

Sam stopped on the top step.

"Who's that?" he said, trying to look back down. "Is that Heather?"

"Nobody! Just keep going!"

We finally made it into the clubhouse. "Ta-da!" I said, using my distracting voice. I even used my distracting arms. "What do you think?" I pointed to the Wall of Fame and the Visitor's Center.

Okay, the bowl of candy.

"What do I *think*?" Sam asked. "I think somebody's calling you, Agnes."

Just then Heather poked her Heather head up through the floor.

"Agnes!" she said, out of breath. "I know you heard me." She put her arm out and shook her head. "Just help me up!"

"Fine," I said, and grabbed her arm.

Sam looked around the place. "It's pretty cool in here," he said, nodding. Then he stopped. And scratched his head. "Wait! Why am I here again? Fudgy didn't really say. He just told me to be sure to bring some slime."

Sam's eyeballs looked at me.

And Heather's did, too.

Then all our eyeballs looked out at the yard.

The rest of the club was arriving, which saved me from answering.

"Hi, guys!" I yelled to the boy part of the club, and Emma.

"We're coming up," Skipper, The Cape, Fudgy, and Emma shouted.

The boy part of the club walked right over to Sam when they got inside.

It was like he *was* magnetized or something!

"You brought some slime, right?" The Cape asked. "Huh? Huh? Did you? Did you?"

Skipper walked over to get some tissues. "Do you know how to blow any other songs besides the national anthem?" he asked. "Here," he said, handing the box to Sam. "You can use these if you want."

"How about that cereal?" Fudgy asked. "Got any more?"

"Careful, careful," I said, trying to get those boys to back up. "Enough with the questions. Don't crowd him. He needs his rest."

Even Sam looked surprised by those words!

"Anyway," I said. "Let's focus." I pulled out my notebook. "I've got some ideas I think will work."

"Ideas?" Fudgy asked. "For *what*?"

I turned to Sam. "For Sam's campaign, that's what."

"My *campaign*?" He shook his head, like he was shaking those words around inside. "*What* campaign?"

I took him over to a beanbag to make him more comfortable.

Plus also, to make sure he didn't faint

when I told him the real reason he was here.

"Oh brother," Fudgy said. "Here we go . . ." He rolled his eyes. "Not another Agnes-saves-the-world project!" He sat down and got himself beanbag comfortable. "Okay, Agnes. Let's hear it."

I got excited eyes. "If you insist . . . First of all, let's all give Sam a huge Secret Knock Club welcome!"

Everyone clapped.

But not in a huge way.

I let it slide.

To get to the important stuff!

"Anyway." I checked the list I'd made in my room before Sam showed up. "First off, we'll need a sign." I sketched something in my book. "Like this," I said, showing everybody.

SUPER SAM the SCIENCE STAR, it said. The *A* in *star* was a real-alive star! "And stickers," I added. "All good campaigns have stickers."

Sam spoke up. "I still don't get it, Agnes. What's all this for?"

"For tomorrow night. At the Science Stars event. We want to help you win. And make us—I mean *you*—famous!"

"No, no, no," Sam said, backing up. "Thanks, but you've already done *way* more than enough!"

He was probably remembering the magnet eyes and rabbit poop.

"I think maybe I liked it better when you weren't talking to me," he said. "It was easier."

Fudgy laughed.

And did his zombie eyes at Skipper.

"How about cereal necklaces then?" I said, looking down at my list. "We could string cereal on rope and make necklaces to hand out."

I looked up to see Sam's face.

It was saying *no*.

"Or, how about a cheer?" I asked, desperate. "You're using Cheerios in your experiment, right?"

"Yeah," he said slowly, like that word was not excited to come out of his mouth.

"So I thought you could use a cheer! Get it? *Cheer*ios."

"I get it," he said. Then he shook his head. I stood up anyway.

"It could go something like this: 'Super Sam the Science Star, do you know how great you are? Floating high above the rest, Super Sam—you are the best!'"

Skipper and The Cape both stood up and went over to check on Sam. "Didn't you hear him, Agnes? He doesn't want any help."

Sam shrugged. "I mean it would be nice if you guys just showed up."

Just showed up!!!

Is he kidding?

How is he going to win if we just show up???

This was not working out!

"Yeah, you know," Sam said, "like for moral support. I mean now that we're great buddies again and all . . ." He sort of laughed when he said those words.

Fudgy put his arm around Sam. "Don't worry, dude. We've got you covered." His eyeballs looked at me as he said the next part. "We'll just show up. *Nothing* else. We promise. Right, guys?"

Everyone nodded.

Even *my* head did.

Only guess what?

Maybe my fingers were busy doing something else.

CHAPTER 9

"HOW DO THESE LOOK?" GRANDMA BLING asked, showing me her earrings.

They were giant dangly stars with rhinestones for the sparkly parts.

"Appropriate, right?" she said, smiling at the mirror.

I nodded.

We were getting ready for the Science Stars night. Mom and Dad had already left for their date night.

Their kissy, smoochy, movie-and-dinner date night.

And here is something strange about that.
They are already married!

"Now what about you?" Grandma Bling said, looking through her jewelry box. "What can we do to bling you up a little?"

I backed up.

'Cause here is some news about bling.

It is not for me!

"Oh, that's right," Grandma Bling said. "What is it your mom and dad always say? Your personality has enough bling already!" She laughed and threw some extra lipstick on her lips.

They looked like Twizzlers!

"Let's go," she said. "Time for the show!" She looked down at the bag in my hands. "Wait. What's all that? I thought you weren't actually *in* the science fair."

"This?" I looked up at her Twizzlered lips. "This is 'just-in-case' stuff."

She sighed. "Should I even ask, Agnes?" She shook her starry ears back and forth.

"Nope," I said, dragging her to the stairs. "I think you should just drive."

The all-purpose room looked dazzling. And sciencey. And starry.

There were sparkle lights on the walls.

For the dazzling part.

Kids at tables with their experiments.

For the sciencey part.

And large cutout stars hanging from the ceiling.

For the starry part.

It felt like a great night to become famous!

There were all kinds of kids representing their classes.

And there was Sam!

His table was all set up.

With his cereal.

And his pellets.

And his bodyguards?

I took a second Agnes look.

Just kidding! It was his parents!

"Could you hold this, please?" I handed Grandma Bling my "just-in-case" bag.

And ran over to Sam's table.

Sam smiled.

I smiled back. "Just here to wish you good

luck, that's all. Nothing else." I looked over at Grandma Bling. And my bag. "At least I hope so," I whispered under my breath. "Oh, and there was something else . . . what was it?" I tapped my feet, like maybe the idea was hiding in my toes. "Oh yes! And to give you moral support. Plain old moral support. Without signs, or stickers, or necklaces, or cheers, or anything. After all, what are friends for?"

I smiled at his parents, too, after my mouth was done being friendly.

"Mom. Dad. *This* is Agnes," Sam said.

This *is Agnes?*

I did not like his tone. But I ignored it.

'Cause I had to check out the competition, that's why!

"See you in a few!" I grabbed Heather and Emma. "Come on. We've got some work to do."

We walked arm in arm around the room, like paper cutout people.

First there was a kid with balloons.

Balloons!

That inflated *without* a mouth blowing them up!

Sam had cereal.

That you couldn't even eat!

"This is not looking good," I possibly said out loud.

"Not looking good?" Heather said. "Are you kidding? This experiment looks great." She read the poster. "'Mix vinegar and baking soda and make carbon dioxide. Enough to inflate a balloon!'"

"I've seen enough to deflate my mood," I

said, pulling away. "Let's see what else there is . . ."

There was an exploring-rock-densities experiment.

And guess what?

I didn't even know what densities were. But it didn't matter.

'Cause they had a real-alive popcorn popper, that's why!

And then we saw it:

The final, put-Agnes-over-the-top experiment.

It measured ball elasticity.

Elasticity is a big word for boingyness.

And it had rubber balls.

And Ping-Pong balls.

And marbles!

Plus also, a lot of kids gathered around.

And some adults who looked like they could be science-fair-judge people.

Something had to be done. And fast!

Sam was never going to win without some help.

But I knew just the Agnes for the job!

CHAPTER 10

"You look tired," I said to Sam, running back to his table. Heather followed me, and Emma followed her. "And possibly sweaty and fevery," I added. I felt his forehead. "You might want to take a little break."

"But I feel fine . . ." Sam said.

"How about the bathroom, then?" I asked. "Do you need to go to the bathroom?"

Sam shook his head.

"Water? How about water? You look like you could be dehydrated."

Sam shook his head again.

I tried his parents. "You must be tired from standing on your feet for so long . . ."

"Well, these shoes *are* a little uncomfortable . . ." Sam's mom said.

BINGO!

"Great! Glad to hear it—I mean . . . I'm very sorry about that." I pointed to the hall. "Why don't you all go and get a bit of fresh air? I don't mind standing here until you get back."

"Oh, no, that's fine," Sam's mom said. "They're not too bad." But just then she looked across the room. "Is that who I think it is?" she said to Sam's dad. She pointed to a lady with a judge sign on her shirt. "Is that Jackie Mills? I can't believe she's a judge here tonight. I used to work with her at the hospital."

She looked at me. "Honey, maybe I *will* take you up on your offer. Are you sure you don't mind manning the booth so Mr. Nash and I can introduce Sam?"

"I'll do better than man the booth," I said. "I'll Agnes the booth! Take as long as you need." I looked at the table. "Don't worry. I've got this place covered."

And she and Sam and Sam's dad all started walking across the room.

This was it!

"Get ready, girls," I said to Heather and Emma. "It's time for Operation Help Sam Win."

I called out to Grandma Bling for my bag. Because:

Props!

That's what Sam's experiment needed.

Nothing *too* much. Just a little sprucing up, that's all!

It wasn't like I was going to change his experiment or anything.

I pulled out an iron.

For the "Ironing Out the Facts" part.

"Um. Agnes? *What* are you doing?" Heather and Emma asked.

And two magnets from my dad's old speakers that I'd found in the garage.

For the magnetized part.

I put them on opposite sides of the table.

Plus also, I unrolled my "just-in-case" poster.

See How MAG-nificent Your Breakfast Cereal Is.

Just then Fudgy, Skipper, and The Cape came running over.

"*What* are you doing, Agnes?" they all said at the same time. "We had a deal, remember?"

"Not now," I said, looking in the bag for my extra spoons. "I don't have much time."

I took the spoons out of the bag and laid them on the table.

CLANK! One of the spoons flew to a magnet.

Then three more flew.

CLANK!

CLANK!

CLANK!

Fudgy picked up the magnet. "Make it stop!" he said.

And then something else happened.

Something that involved the *other* magnet.

And the iron.

CLAAAANNNK!

They collided!

And so did two ladies when they heard the CLANK!

"Seriously, Agnes," Fudgy said. "Make this stop." He grabbed the iron.

And the ladies grabbed Skipper.

And all three fell to the ground.

Heather and Emma ran around to the front of table.

Just as Sam's cereal bowls fell.

Onto the two ladies' heads.

Plus also, Skipper's.

Which just happened to be right when Super Sam walked back with his parents and Judge Mills.

There is a word for what we all looked like: *Suspicious.*

I glanced at Super Sam's face.

It was super sad!

But it wasn't quite as sad then as it was later when the judges announced who was going on to regionals.

And Sam's name wasn't called.

CHAPTER 11

"YOU CAN'T STAY UNDER THERE FOREVER."

The next morning I was in my bed.

With the covers over my head.

I was like an Agnes ghost!

A ghost who was very, very, very, *very* sorry for Sam.

"You're going to have to come out and talk about this *sometime*," Dad continued, trying to pull back the sheets. I'm pretty sure his voice also wanted to say, "What exactly were you thinking, Agnes?" but it stopped itself.

I poked my hand out and pointed to my sign.

My *DO NOT DISTURB* sign.

Plus also, the one that said *CLOSED FOR BUSINESS*.

Grandma Bling chuckled. "Look, honey, I know things didn't go *exactly* as planned last night . . ." I shook my ghost head. "But you're going to have to come out and face the music."

"Music?" I mumbled. "I don't deserve any music."

And then I possibly also cried.

Although here is some good news about being a ghost.

Nobody can see when your eyeballs leak!

"We know you were only trying to help Sam and everything . . ."

"That's just it, Grandma!" I finally pulled back the sheets and sat up. "That's not really—" I stopped myself before I said "true."

Grandma Bling hugged me. "Oh dear,"

she said. "I'm sensing this might be a Fixer-Upper?"

I nodded. "Big time," I said.

Most people think a Fixer-Upper is a house. But not Grandma Bling!

She says a Fixer-Upper is somebody whose feelings need fixing up.

"I know just the thing to help," she said, looking at me and Mom and Dad. "I've been baking since early this morning, and you know what one of my chocolate cakes can do, right? It can cure almost anything." She turned to me and winked. "Or *anyone*."

"I'm here to cure Sam," I said to his mom when she answered the door.

Grandma Bling was waiting in the car. I turned around. She gave me a wink and a thumbs-up for good luck.

"Cure him?" she said, looking puzzled. "But he's not sick, honey." She stopped for a minute. "Wait. You're Agnes, right? From last night?"

And just then I did not want to be "Agnes from last night."

I wanted to be "Agnes from right now" who was going to fix up Sam's feelings.

"Is Sam here?" I asked, looking over her shoulder. "I'd like to give him this."

I held out Grandma Bling's chocolate cake. "It cures anything and anyone!" I said. I looked down at the ground when I said the next part. "Especially people who didn't make it to regionals."

"Sam!" his mom called out. "Agnes is here to cure you . . ." She shook her head. "I mean see you."

Sam started walking down the stairs.

I gulped.

"Hey," he said.

"Hey," I said back.

"Why don't you two go into the kitchen and have a slice of that cake?" his mom said. "I'll be there in a few minutes."

I followed Sam into the kitchen.

"I'm really sorry," I blurted out before we even sat down. I took a chunk of the cake and shoved it in his mouth. "Here. This will help."

Sam wiped away the crumbs.

"What was *that* for?" he said.

"That's to make you feel better," I said. "And to say I'm sorry. Really, really, really, really, REALLY sorry."

He brushed some more crumbs off. "It's okay, Agnes," he said. "I know you were just trying to help . . ."

Has he been talking to Grandma Bling?
And why is he being so nice??

He is making this even harder!

"But that's just it, Sam," I said, shoving some cake in my own mouth so maybe my words would sound sweeter. "I wasn't just trying to help—well, not just you at least. I was trying to help you win so we could all be famous. I know it sounds silly, but after we lost the spelling bee I wanted to win something. And I thought you could be the one to make us famous. You know, Mrs. Duncan's Famous Room Five Science Stars!" I put my head on the kitchen counter. "We were going to be in the newspaper and everything!"

"If it makes you feel any better," he said, trying to find one of my eyeballs under my hair, "the judge said I wouldn't have won. With or *without* your help. That other kid's project was amazing."

Wait? Really? He wouldn't have won?

But that wasn't the point!

The point was Sam was a seriously super nice guy.

A seriously super nice guy I wanted to call my friend.

I had to do something to make it up to him!

But what?

And just then my brain got smacked on the inside with the perfect idea.

If Sam couldn't go to regionals, maybe regionals could come to him!

We could have our own science fair regionals. In my backyard! And even camp outside!

We could call it The Secret Knock Club and the Great Sleep-Under . . . the Stars!

And the main attraction?

Super Sam the Science *Star*!

I couldn't wait to tell the rest of the club!

CHAPTER 12

"WE DON'T HAVE TO SING?" FUDGY ASKED.

"Or play an instrument?" Skipper asked.

"Or clean anything up?" Heather said.

"Or go to a retirement home?" The Cape and Emma asked.

They were running down the list of all the community-service projects we'd done as The Secret Knock Club.

I shook my head at all of them.

"It'll all be right here," I said, looking out the clubhouse window. "Sciencey stuff. Good-food stuff. Tent stuff. Sleeping-under-the stars stuff. My parents said they were okay with it all. Especially since we owe Sam . . ."

"*We* owe Sam?" Fudgy said. "Don't you mean—"

"Okay, fine!" I interrupted. "Since *I* owe Sam."

Fudgy nodded. "Then I guess we're in this time," he said. "A sleep-*under* does sound pretty cool." He did a scary voice. "I just hope nobody's afraid of the dark!"

I started going down my checklist.

"We should invite the whole class, right?"

"Yep," they all agreed.

Plus also, I added Mrs. Duncan and Mrs. Elliott, our science teacher, to that list.

"And keep it a surprise for Sam, right?"

They all agreed again.

I wrote down a little note. It said: *Tell Sam's parents. Not Sam.* "I'll make the invitations and we'll pass them out at school without Sam seeing. Sound good?"

"Sounds good," everyone replied.

"Oh, and who has a tent?" I asked.

Fudgy, Skipper, and Emma all raised their hands.

"We've got two huge ones for our family camping trips," Emma said. "I'm sure my parents would let us use them."

I checked *Tent* off my list.

"And what about a sign?" I asked. "We'll need something to put up." We all looked at The Cape after I said those words.

"Hey," he said, laughing. "I've *got* to do it. It's tradition!"

I checked *Sign* off the list, too.

And then put a worried face by that tradition.

"Fine," I said, "but is it okay if I make the flyers this time? Just to be safe."

He nodded. Check.

"And tables . . ." I called out, still going down the list.

"We have a bunch from Girl Scouts," Heather said. "I'm sure we could use them."

This was coming together!

The first-ever "I'm sorry, Sam" Secret Knock Club Science Fair Regionals.

In my backyard region!

"I think we forgot something," Skipper said. "When are we going to do it?"

"Good point," I said. I thought for a second. "How about the day of the real-alive regionals? April seventh. That way Sam won't feel too bad about not being there." Everyone nodded. "I'll just double-check with my parents, but I'm sure it will be fine. They said anytime in the next two weeks would be okay."

And then I remembered something else when I said that date.

I had a cancellation to make!

"I'll be right back, guys," I said. "I have to cancel our fame."

"Grandma," I said, holding up the telephone when I got inside, "would you be able to dial the newspaper reporter person for me, please? I'm afraid I have some bad news for her."

Grandma Bling agreed and called the newspaper.

"Here she is," Grandma Bling said, handing me the phone.

"I need to cancel you, Ms. Ellen Marker," I said very nicely.

"Who is this?" she asked.

"Oh, sorry," I said, forgetting my newspaper manners. "This is Agnes Mary Murphy from Lakeview Elementary School. We don't need you for the science fair regionals anymore. Super Sam the Science Star won't be there after all."

"Really?" she said. "That's unfortunate. What happened?"

"How much time do you have?" I asked.

"How about the short version?"

"Well, the short version is he didn't make it. Actually, he was . . ." *What was that word Fudgy used?* "Sabotaged!"

Sabotaged is a big word for trying to help even if it didn't seem like it.

"Sabotaged?" she said, sounding surprised. "That sounds serious. Who would do something like that?"

I told her I was the someone who would do something like that. And then I told her we were having our own regionals to make up for it. Same day. Same time. Different place.

"Wait?" she said, continuing. "Just so I

have this right . . . you mean you're putting together a whole event just to say sorry to your friend?"

She called Sam my friend!

I nodded.

And then said yes since she couldn't see me.

"Then I don't think there's anything we need to cancel," she said. "This sounds like an event I would love to cover. You know . . . friendship . . . kindness . . . saying 'I'm sorry.' It's the sort of thing people love to read about."

"They do?" I said, surprised. "I mean of course they do!" Then I jumped up and down. "Wait! Does that mean you're coming to my real-alive backyard? With a reporter pencil? And reporter notebook and everything?"

"It looks like it," Ms. Ellen Marker said. "And probably a reporter camera, too," she said, chuckling. I nearly fainted at those words! "I'm still going to the other regionals as well, but I think I'll have time to swing by your event first. Trust me, these kind of stories melt people's hearts."

And just then my heart felt like it was going to do something, too.

Stop!

CHAPTER 13

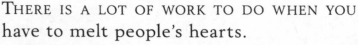

THERE IS A LOT OF WORK TO DO WHEN YOU have to melt people's hearts.

First up?

Pass out invitations without Sam's eyeballs seeing.

"Don't you need to go to the bathroom or something?" I asked him. "You might want to go before math starts."

Sam looked suspicious. "The last time you asked me if I had to go to the bathroom . . ."

"Ha!" I said, laughing. I pretended to check my pockets. "Look, no irons or anything!" I smiled. "Promise!"

I eyeballed Fudgy for some help.

"Hey, Sam," he said, holding up a ball. It was our silent speed ball for indoor recess.

"Mrs. Duncan said we could go and give this to Ms. Cray in the gym before the bell rings." He nodded. "Coming? We've got to be back before the announcements."

Sam shrugged. "Sure. I guess."

And they left the room.

So I could make an Agnes announcement!

"Mrs. Duncan?" I looked over at her desk. "Is now okay?"

She nodded. "Sure, go ahead."

My parents and I had run the idea by her already, and she said it sounded fabulous!

Plus also, she was going to come with Mrs. Elliott!

I cleared my throat. "Fellow science supporters," I said, standing in front of the room.

Nobody looked up.

I tried a joke.

"How do astronomers organize a party?" I said, with a little louder Agnes voice.

It worked! I had an audience.

"They planet!" I said, laughing. "And we've planned something, too." I walked up and down the rows handing out the invitations.

Here's what they said:

THE
SECRET KNOCK CLUB
invites you to support
SUPER SAM THE SCIENCE STAR!
It's a Sleep-Under . . . the stars.
(NOT SAM THE STAR, THE REAL-
ALIVE TWINKLE STARS!!)
I'M

At the first-ever "we're-
really-sorry-for-what-happened"
Science Fair Regionals.

In our backyard region.

April 7th.
325 Wheatfield Way

SHHH! IT'S A SURPRISE!

Mrs. Duncan raised her hand.

"I have a question," she said. "Just so everyone is clear about something. What kind of science are you going to showcase? You know . . . astronomy? Geology?"

"Oh, we'll take any kind," I said. "Fun science. Boring science. Whatever you want. You could bring your own experiment or just come and see ours. We'll be doing some fun stuff." I paused. "And we'll all check out Sam's experiment, too, of course." I smiled. "Without me butting in."

She chuckled.

And then she didn't get to say anything else.

'Cause Fudgy and Sam walked back in.

"Mission accomplished," I whispered in Fudgy's ear.

Then I looked down at my list.

Second up?

Building a Super-Sam-the-Science-Star Stage in my backyard after school.

CHAPTER 14

"CHECK THE MAP," FUDGY SAID. "THIS LOOKS about right to me."

Fudgy was standing in the middle of the yard.

I rolled out the map we'd drawn to double-check the layout of everything for the sleep-under.

We looked like treasure hunters!

In the middle was Sam's stage.

And in a circle around it were the other tables.

"Yep, looks good," I said. "Now we just need to wait for Bob the Builder. He's changing his clothes."

And here's some funny news about that.

My dad's real-alive name is Bob.

So that's what we call him when he helps us build stuff.

Bob the Builder!

Fudgy reached into a bag of chips. "No problem," he said. "I've got time *on* my hands. And chips *in* them! I'm not going anywhere."

And he crunched and munched away until Bob the Builder showed up.

"Now, let's see what you kids have in mind," he said, looking at the map.

His eyes got builder big. "Is that a? . . ."

I looked over his shoulder.

"Yep," I said, smiling. "A star platform. For Sam to stand on."

"And these are? . . ."

"Oh, those are poles, so we can hang the sign above him."

Bob wiped his forehead. "Wow," he said. "This looks like it could take a few days to build." Then he turned to us and smiled. "But I've got the time if you do."

And we did! We were all chipping in.

So for the next three days Bob chopped.

And we carried.

And Bob cut.

And we dragged.

And Bob sawed.

And we pulled.

And Bob hammered.

And we watched.

And ate more chips.

Until finally we had a Super-Sam-the-Science-Star Stage. And it looked super awesome!

I did a big Agnes smile at that stage.

And gave Bob a big Agnes hug.

Then it was time to plan for the rest of the yard.

We cut out huge stars to hang from the trees.

Other sciencey people use beakers to mix their science experiment stuff in. But not us!

We made "beakers" for everyone to wear.

Pelican ones.

And toucan ones.

Hummingbird ones.

And woodpecker ones.

Plus also, we were going to wear belts.

Asteroid belts!

Grandma Bling told us about those.

"You've heard of comets, right?" She was tying the last piece of string on one of our woodpecker beakers.

We nodded.

"Well, asteroids are very similar. They're made of rock and metal. And they're found in a part of our solar system called the asteroid belt. It's between Mars and Jupiter."

Grandma Bling sounded like a professional asteroid expert!

She walked over to a cupboard and pulled out a huge pile of felt. "You can cut strips of this," she said, adding some Velcro to the ends, "and then glue some of these on." She held up a Styrofoam ball. "Ta-da!" she said,

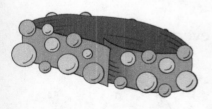 putting it around her waist. "You've got your-self an asteroid belt!"

We all started cutting strips of felt.

"Of course," Grandma Bling said, wink-ing, "you can always add a little *bling* if you want." And *poof*! Suddenly she had a glittery asteroid belt!

Before you know it, we had enough belts for everyone.

Then Grandma Bling showed us one more thing.

She walked over to the calendar and ripped off the front page.

The one that said April 6.

"Look what tomorrow is!" she said, with an excited Grandma Bling voice. "Your big day!"

CHAPTER 15

I STARED AT THE SIGN ABOVE THE STAGE.

"SCAR?" I said, very out loud. "The science *scar*? Are you kidding me? Not again!"

Ms. Ellen Marker and her reporter camera were on their way to see a science *scar*?

I looked around the place. "Where's The Cape?" I said, also very out loud.

Everything else was done.

We'd set up the tents.

Put out the tables.

Set up our experiments.

Hung up the stars.

Put out the food.

And now *this*? And just when everyone was starting to show up!

A kid named Jack came with his experiment. "It's about the relationship between earthworms and light," he said.

Heather heard the earthworms part. "You can go and set up over there," she said, pointing to the other side of the yard. "WAY over there."

"Cool," Jack said.

And he left with his earthworms.

Plus also, his pelican beaker and belt.

Then came a girl named Sophia. Her experiment looked like a piece of paper in a bottle.

"It's invisible ink . . . with lemon juice," she whispered. "I'll just need to run inside and maybe borrow your hair dryer or something to heat it up so everyone can see the message."

Heather said the invisible ink could go wherever Sophia wanted.

Then even more kids came with their experiments.

And Mrs. Duncan and Mrs. Elliott showed up.

And before you know it, the place was full!

"Hey, where's the scar?" asked a group of

boys. The kids started laughing. They were looking up at the stage.

I checked my watch. "He'll be here in fifteen minutes," I said, not laughing. "We've *got* to do something about that sign!"

And just then The Cape ran up to the stage. And ripped the sign in half!

And here's some news about that.

Behind it was another sign.

A real-alive sign that said *SUPER SAM THE SCIENCE STAR*.

"Ha!" he said, laughing. "Fooled you!" He smiled at his joke. "You didn't think I would mess up *again*, did you?"

But I didn't get to answer. 'Cause just then two more people showed up.

One was early.

His name was Sam.

And one was on time.

Her name was newspaper reporter Ms. Ellen Marker.

"Surprise!" I screamed at the Sam part.

"Surprise!" everyone else screamed, too.

Super Sam looked super confused.

Newspaper reporter Ellen Marker looked delighted.

And started taking newspaper pictures with her camera!

"What's going on?" Sam asked, hiding from the flash. "Mom and Dad said we were just stopping by to pick up another one of your grandma's cakes."

"You are," I said. "A congratulations cake. But that's for later . . ."

He still looked super confused.

"First, you're having a surprise science fair! Your very own science fair regionals! Here. In our backyard region." I explained a little more. "It's kind of like a surprise party, only no gifts."

I showed him around the place.

"And this," I said, taking him to the stage, "is where you'll get to do your experiment for all of us." I looked into his Sam eyeballs. "Without any Agnes interference for once . . ."

Sam took a deep breath. "You guys did this for *me*?" There was maybe a little eye leak when he said those words. "*Why?*"

"To say sorry for ruining your chances of the real-alive regionals," I said. "Plus also, 'cause we really like you!"

"I don't know what to say." Sam put his hands near his eyeballs, which looked like they were starting to leak again.

"I do!" I said, handing him a woodpecker beaker and an asteroid belt. "Say you'll put this stuff on and come show us your experiment. Check it out—your parents already set it up!"

Then I handed him a lab coat.

'Cause a science star should look even more sciencey and starry than everyone else, that's why!

And I walked him to his stage.

CHAPTER 16

SAM GULPED.

He was up on the stage.

By himself.

We were all sitting down in the audience.

No magnet eyes. No rabbit poop. No irons. Nothing!

Just plain old sitting.

And watching.

And waiting . . .

And watching . . .

And waiting . . .

And . . . *Is that something moving under the table?*

I shook my head.

Probably just the wind, I thought.

Sam gulped again. "Ummm . . ." he started to say.

He looked over at Ms. Ellen Marker.

She had her reporter pencil and note-book out.

"I don't think I can . . ." Sam started to say.

Then something moved again.

And this time I saw it.

It was Rat-A-Tat.

Rat-A-Tat was on the loose!

And on the prowl for Super Sam's cereal.

Great! This time I wasn't going to ruin Sam's experiment.

My cat was!

And then I realized something else.

Sam wasn't answering because he had reporter fright!

It was a double whammy of bad.

I have to do something!

But just then Sam finally spoke.

And he asked me to join him on the stage. "Agnes?" he said. "Will you come up and help me?"

I turned around to see if there was another Agnes. Maybe one who didn't sabo-tage things. And cause widespread panic.

But then I realized: I was the Agnes he was asking.

"Me?" I dashed up to the stage. "Why me?" I asked, looking around for Rat-A-Tat.

"Because you're my friend," he whispered. "And I'd like your help."

"My help?" I said. My voice quivered when I saw Rat-A-Tat. "Of course. My help!"

Rat-A-Tat took a leap out from under the table.

Sam didn't see.

But where did she go?

"Here," Sam said, handing me a paper.

I looked at the paper and then looked around for Rat-A-Tat again.

And then I did what any friend would do.

While Sam showed the experiment, I said the words he told me to say.

Words like *duct tape* . . .

And *magnets* . . .

And *combine things in a blender* . . .

And . . .

"RAT-A-TAT!"

"What did you say, Agnes?" Sam looked confused. "That's a wrap?" He looked around at the experiment. "We're not done yet." And he continued to mix and pour and science things up.

I laughed. "Silly me!" I said, and I looked up to see Rat-A-Tat hanging down from the Science Star sign. "Of course we're not done."

Everyone in the audience started to laugh. And point. And gasp.

"It looks like they like the experiment," Sam said, smiling.

Rat-A-Tat's paw tried to reach down.

"Sure does," I said, panicking.

And I reached up and pulled Rat-A-Tat down to safety.

On my head!

Sam turned around.

He shook his head. "When did that happen?"

"Don't ask," I said.

And he didn't have time to

because just then Ms. Ellen Marker started taking pictures.

Lots and lots of pictures.

For the NEWSPAPER!

And maybe—okay, definitely—Rat-A-Tat's paws were in my eyes for most of them.

Everyone clapped for Sam's experiment.

And whooped!

And hollered!

And then we all went around to look at the other experiments and the fun stations we'd set up.

Like the Meteor Shower.

Only it was a "meat-ier" shower. Where you had to catch pieces of chicken and beef in your mouth.

And the Shooting Stars target range.

Where you had to launch a rubber band and hit one of the hanging stars.

Mrs. Duncan and Mrs. Elliott were both very impressed.

Even if maybe some of the rubber bands flew into their hair.

And even if they got a little messy at our cake walk. Where you had to walk in real-alive cake!

"You've done such a great job here today," Mrs. Duncan said to all of us. She and Mrs. Elliott looked over at Sam. He was catching chicken in his mouth and laughing away. "We know The Secret Knock Club usually does community-service projects, but sometimes raising somebody's spirits can be just as important. And I think we can all agree you accomplished that today!"

And it was true!

Sam said our backyard regionals event was way better than any regular regionals could have been.

Even if it did start to rain before we could sleep out under the stars.

But the good news is we did get to sleep out under something.

My back porch!

And here's even more good news about that.

We were closer to the newspaper in the morning when Grandma Bling brought it out.

And guess whose picture was in there?

All of ours!

Mrs. Duncan.

Mrs. Elliott.

Grandma Bling.

Mom and Dad.

Our class.

And The Secret Knock Club.

Including me!

And the best news of all?

It also included the newest member of the club.

Super Sam the Science Star!

Local Students Bring
Classroom to the Backyard

Pg. 23

DO YOU WANT TO BE MORE LIKE THE SECRET KNOCK CLUB? HERE ARE TEN COMMUNITY-SERVICE PROJECTS YOU CAN DO!

1. Start a food drive. NO, I don't mean your food will actually drive. (Imagine a can of soup driving a car!) Have your friends and family, your neighbors, and your school contribute canned food and donate it to a homeless shelter.

2. Start a community garden. (Composting is optional!)

3. Write cards to kids who are in the hospital.

4. Or create "busy books" for kids who are in the hospital, to keep them entertained and laughing! No, the book isn't busy. But the kid who gets it will be! The books could include jokes, mazes and other games, comic strips, and more!

5. Clean up your environment. Pick up litter along a stream, around your school, or anywhere you find it. Remember, always have an adult accompany you!

6. Donate new or gently used stuffed animals to your local fire department to help kids who might be scared in an emergency situation.

7. Bake some tasty treats for a local senior center. Remember that some people have allergies, though, so label them with the ingredients!

8. Set up a lemonade stand in your neighborhood and donate the proceeds to a local charity of your choice.

9. Help an elderly neighbor with some simple chores.

10. Volunteer at your local animal shelter.

ABOUT THE AUTHOR

Louise Bonnett-Rampersaud was born in England and moved to the United States when she was six. She has lived in Florida, Pennsylvania, and Maryland. She received a journalism degree from the University of Maryland. In addition to The Secret Knock Club series, Louise is also the author of *Polly Hopper's Pouch*, illustrated by Lina Chesak-Liberace; *How Do You Sleep?*, illustrated by Kristin Kest; *Bubble & Squeak*, illustrated by Susan Banta; and *Never Ask a Bear*, illustrated by Doris Barrette. She lives in Maryland with her family.

ABOUT THE ILLUSTRATOR

Adam McHeffey is a musician as well as an author and illustrator. He graduated with a BA from SUNY Purchase College and currently lives in Nashville, Tennessee. Adam is both the writer and illustrator of two picture books: *Asiago*, which *School Library Journal* called "funny and fresh," and *Rudy and Claude Splash Into Art*. He is also the illustrator of The Secret Knock Club chapter-book series. Learn more about him and his work at www.adammcheffey.com.

A SECRET KNOCK GETS YOU INTO THE CLUBHOUSE!

Join Agnes and her friends in The Secret Knock Club as they help with community-service projects.

Book #1, The Dyno-Mite Dog Show: The Secret Knock Club is doing a community-service project at the Brookside Retirement Village. But will the dog show (and canine wedding) be a success? Or a dog-gone disaster?

Book #2, The Spring Un-Fair: The members of The Secret Knock Club decide to raise money to rent a dunk tank for the spring fair by putting on a rock concert. But can any of the club members play instruments or sing?

Book #3, Going Green: The Secret Knock Club teams up with kindergarten buddies to create a new reading space at school. But will they get everything done in time for the opening ceremony and a visit by a famous author?